Little Princesses
The Fairytale Princess

www.kidsatrandomhouse.co.uk/littleprincesses

THE *Little Princesses* SERIES
The Whispering Princess
The Fairytale Princess
The Peach Blossom Princess
The Rain Princess

And look out for more
adventures coming soon!
The Snowflake Princess
The Dream-catcher Princess
The Desert Princess
The Lullaby Princess

Little Princesses
The Fairytale Princess

By Katie Chase

Illustrated by Leighton Noyes

Red Fox

Special thanks to Narinder Dhami

THE FAIRYTALE PRINCESS

A RED FOX BOOK 978 0 099 48829 3 (from January 2007)

0 099 48829 9

First published in Great Britain by Red Fox,
an imprint of Random House Children's Books

This edition published 2006

1 3 5 7 9 10 8 6 4 2

Series created by Working Partners Ltd
Copyright © Working Partners Ltd, 2006
Illustrations copyright © Leighton Noyes, 2006
Cover illustration by Nila Aye

Papers used by Random House Children's Books are natural, recyclable products
made from wood grown in sustainable forests. The manufacturing processes conform
to the environmental regulations of the country of origin.

Set in 15/21pt Bembo Schoolbook

Red Fox Books are published by Random House Children's Books,
61–63 Uxbridge Road, London W5 5SA,
a division of The Random House Group Ltd,
in Australia by Random House Australia (Pty) Ltd,
20 Alfred Street, Milsons Point, Sydney, NSW 2061, Australia,
in New Zealand by Random House New Zealand Ltd,
18 Poland Road, Glenfield, Auckland 10, New Zealand,
and in South Africa by Random House (Pty) Ltd,
Isle of Houghton, Corner Boundary Road & Carse O'Gowrie,
Houghton 2198, South Africa

THE RANDOM HOUSE GROUP Limited Reg. No. 954009
www.kidsatrandomhouse.co.uk

A CIP catalogue record for this book is available from the British Library.

Printed and bound in Great Britain by Cox & Wyman Ltd, Reading, Berkshire

For Tonia Coney,
a dear cousin and a dear friend

Chapter One

Rosie stood as still as she could behind the heavy velvet curtain. She could hear footsteps coming along the corridor towards her.

"Got you!" Rosie's little brother Luke pulled the curtain aside and grinned at her. "My turn to hide now."

"How did you know I was there?" Rosie laughed as they turned and walked back towards the Great Hall.

"I saw your trainers sticking out under the curtain," Luke replied.

"Now, I'm going to find a really *brilliant* place to hide."

"Go on, then," Rosie said with a smile, turning away to face the roaring fire in the huge stone fireplace of the Great Hall and enjoying the heat from the orange flames. The castle could sometimes feel very cold now that it was autumn.

"Count to one hundred, Rosie, and no cheating," Luke ordered.

"What a cheek!" Rosie replied. "I *never* cheat!" She began to count. "One, two, three . . ."

Rosie heard Luke's footsteps disappear into the distance as he raced out of the Great Hall. As she counted higher, Rosie thought how lucky she and Luke were. Not many people got the chance to play hide-and-seek in a *real* castle!

The castle in the Scottish Highlands belonged to Rosie's Great-aunt Rosamund, who loved to travel. She had been all over the world, collecting curious treasures and antiques, which now furnished the castle.

At the moment, she was away for two years on another trip, so she'd asked Rosie and her family if they would move in and look after her home while she was gone. Rosie was thrilled. She loved her great-aunt, who always called Rosie her "Little Princess", and the castle was one of her favourite places in the whole world. It wasn't quite the same without Great-aunt Rosamund around, but she had left behind a wonderful secret for Rosie to discover.

"Forty-nine, fifty, fifty-one . . ."

Rosie glanced around the enormous room. Wherever she went in the castle, she was always on the lookout for little princesses. Her great-aunt had told her that they were hidden all around the castle, and they could be anywhere: a tiny figure painted on a vase, a tall statue made of marble, or even a picture on a rug! Part of the fun for Rosie was not knowing where she would find the next one.

"Eighty-eight, eighty-nine, ninety . . ."

Rosie wondered where she should start looking for her brother. She glanced up at the ceiling. Maybe Luke had gone into one of the bedrooms to hide.

As she stared upwards, Rosie's gaze fell on the large tapestry that hung above the fireplace. It had been part of the Great Hall for so long, she almost didn't notice it any more. But now, a feeling of huge excitement rushed through her.

The picture showed a girl in a flowing, blue medieval gown with a gold sash around her waist. On her head was a pointed blue hat with a white veil that hung down over her long blonde hair.

To one side of the girl stood a golden dragon. He looked very fierce, with sharp teeth and claws and golden scales. His mouth was open and a stream of orange and red

flames poured from it. On the
other side of the girl, a knight
in shining silver armour sat, tall
and proud, on a white horse.

"She must be a little
princess!" Rosie said to herself,
staring hard at the girl in the
tapestry. "She looks a bit scared.

But I'd be scared too if I was standing right next to a dragon!"

Rosie forgot all about Luke and their game of hide-and-seek. Remembering the instructions in her great-aunt's letter, she took a deep breath and bobbed down into a low curtsey. "Hello!" she said, her eyes fixed on the girl in the blue dress.

No sooner had the word left her lips than a soft breeze rustled through the Great Hall. Rosie felt herself wrapped in a warm whirlwind that smelled faintly of summer fields and wild flowers. It lifted her gently off her feet, as Rosie closed her eyes and waited to see what would happen. Was she about to meet a little princess?

Just a moment or two later, Rosie felt her feet touch down again on soft, springy grass. The smell of summer meadows, flowers and hay was stronger now and she could feel the warmth of the sun on her skin.

Rosie opened her eyes and gasped in wonder. She was standing in the countryside on a beautiful summer's day. The scene around her was like a picture in a fairytale. The sky overhead was a deep blue, studded with tiny white clouds. All around her were meadows dotted with flowers, fields of rippling golden corn and rolling green hills stretching away in every direction.

"This is *lovely!*" Rosie sighed happily.

Then, for the first time, she noticed that her clothes had changed too. Instead of her jeans and sweatshirt, she was now wearing a long, golden medieval dress with a pointed gold hat and white veil.

Rosie smiled. She was just smoothing
down her dress and admiring her dainty
golden slippers, when she heard a strange
noise above her head.

Flap! Flap! Flap!

Rosie looked upwards, and immediately screamed. The golden dragon from the tapestry was flying straight towards her, and he looked very real!

"Go away!" Rosie shouted, waving her arms. But to her horror, the creature opened his mouth, ready to send his fiery breath shooting straight at her. The dragon was going to burn Rosie to a crisp!

Chapter Two

Rosie couldn't move. She stared at the
dragon, her eyes wide with terror, and waited
to feel flames surround her. But suddenly,
something struck her hard on her right
shoulder, knocking her over and out of
the way. She rolled across the grass and sat
up in a muddy patch.

"Oh, please forgive me," said an anxious
voice beside her. "I didn't mean to knock you
over. But I had to get you out of the way!"

Cautiously Rosie looked round. The
dragon had gone and next to her sat the

princess in the blue dress from the tapestry.
A trail of blackened grass marked the spot
where Rosie had been standing only
moments before. And the charred grass led to
a small tree that was still burning brightly.

"Are you all right?" the girl asked
anxiously. "Have you hurt yourself?"

Rosie shook her head. She was fine, but
her dress was rather muddy.

"What's your name?" the girl asked, helping Rosie to her feet and trying to brush the mud off her dress. "I haven't seen you around the village before. I'm Princess Isabella."

"*Princess* Isabella?" Rosie repeated excitedly.

Isabella nodded, looking puzzled, so Rosie tried to explain. "I'm Rosie," she said. "I saw you in a tapestry in my great-aunt's castle, and I curtseyed and said 'Hello,' and here I am!"

Isabella's blue eyes lit up. "Of course!" she gasped. "It's magic!"

Rosie nodded.

"My grandmother told me stories about a friend who used to visit her by magic when she was a little girl," Isabella went on. "My grandmother's friend was called Rosamund."

"That's my great-aunt!" Rosie laughed.

"Then we shall be friends, too!" Isabella declared imperiously. "Welcome to the kingdom of Tannelaun." She waved her hand at the fields and meadows. Then she smiled and rushed on excitedly, "Do you like it? Isn't it beautiful? My father's castle isn't far away, but you can't see it because it's just behind that hill. And just by the castle is the village. And the sea is over there, beyond those fields. And if you look . . ."

Rosie blinked and opened her mouth to speak, but she couldn't get a word in. She tugged at her friend's sleeve instead, and couldn't help noticing that there wasn't a speck of mud on Isabella's blue dress. But then, she *was* a little princess!

"Sorry," Isabella laughed. "My father says I could talk the legs off a cooking pot!"

"I just wanted to say thank you for saving my life," Rosie said gratefully. "I was so scared when I saw that dragon flying towards me! Does he live in Tannelaun? Is he terrorizing the kingdom? Can't you get rid of him somehow?"

To Rosie's astonishment, Isabella immediately looked very upset. Her face fell, her shoulders slumped and tears appeared in her eyes.

"What's the matter?" Rosie asked anxiously.

"Oh, Rosie," Isabella sighed. "The dragon isn't really fierce at all. He's called Cedric, and he's my pet!"

Chapter Three

"Wow!" Rosie said in amazement. "You have a dragon for a pet?"

"It's rather strange, I know," Isabella replied, wiping her eyes. "Most people have a cat or a dog."

"I thought dragons only existed in story books," Rosie said curiously.

Isabella looked shocked. "Of course not," she replied. "They're everywhere! But usually they live in the wild. I don't know anyone else who has a pet dragon."

"I think that's fantastic!" Rosie breathed,

beaming at her new friend. Having a dragon for a pet was the coolest thing she'd ever heard. "Where did you find Cedric?"

"In that cave, over there," Isabella said, pointing to an opening at the foot of a hill. "He'd just hatched out of a golden egg."

"What happened to his parents?" Rosie asked.

Isabella shrugged. "I don't know," she said. "But I couldn't leave him all alone, so I begged and begged my father to let me keep him. At last he said yes, so Cedric came to live in the castle with us."

Rosie's eyes opened wide. Imagine having a dragon living in your house!

"Oh, but Cedric's very sweet and loving," Isabella said quickly. "He wasn't any trouble." She sighed. "Until he got bigger, that is, and began sharpening his claws on my father's throne!"

"So what happened then?" asked Rosie.

"Well, he was just too big for the castle. He was knocking over all the furniture," Isabella explained, "so he had to move back to his cave. It's much better for him because there's more room, and he still comes down to the village to visit me – but that's the problem! Cedric gets very nervous around everyone except me. And when he gets nervous, he gets the hiccups. And when he gets the hiccups, he can't control his fiery breath!"

"Oh, dear," said Rosie with a frown. "So Cedric wasn't aiming at me just now?"

Isabella shook her head. "No, I was trying to train him to control his fire-breathing. Look!" She pointed at a target painted on a nearby rock. "He was trying to hit that, but he hasn't quite managed it yet."

"Yes, I can see that!" Rosie said with a smile, glancing at the unscathed target and then at the scorched tree.

"He's had so many accidents," Isabella sighed. "My father's annoyed because last week Cedric burned up his favourite table. And the villagers are always complaining about him. The butcher had to push his cart into the village pond last week because Cedric had accidentally set it alight!"

The little princess looked so upset that Rosie felt very sorry for her. "Don't worry," she said comfortingly. "I'm sure that Cedric will soon learn to control his fire-breathing."

"You haven't heard the worst part yet," Isabella went on miserably. "My father says that if Cedric doesn't stop setting things on fire, he'll have to be sent away!"

That made Rosie miserable too, because it was clear that Isabella really loved her pet dragon very much. "Where's Cedric now?" she asked, looking round.

"He flew into his cave to hide," Isabella explained. "I think you scared him."

Rosie laughed. "*I* scared *him*?" she said. "Imagine a *dragon* being scared of *me*! Can I say hello to him?"

Isabella's face lit up. "Yes, here he comes now." She pointed at the cave. "Cedric, come and meet Rosie."

The dragon was peering shyly out of his cave, his large brown eyes a little worried. He stared at Rosie for a few moments before

creeping cautiously towards the girls, his
wings folded neatly on his back. He stopped
in front of Isabella, bent his large golden
head and nuzzled her shoulder.

Isabella stroked his ears and smiled at
Rosie. "Rosie, this is Cedric. Cedric, this
is Rosie," she said.

Rosie felt very small beside the huge dragon.
She reached out and patted his head.
The golden scales felt warm
and smooth, like silk.

"I'm very pleased to
meet you, Cedric,"
she said with a
grin.

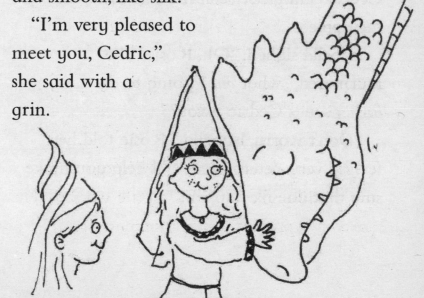

Cedric looked pleased too. He made a rumbling sound of contentment; Rosie thought it sounded just like the purring of a gigantic cat.

"He likes you," Isabella said, dipping a hand into the pocket of her dress and pulling out an apple. "He won't be nervous around you now, so you don't have to worry about any fiery hiccups!"

"He's lovely," Rosie beamed, scratching Cedric gently between his ears as he ate the apple.

Isabella sighed. "Oh, Rosie," she murmured, "what *am* I going to do if my father sends Cedric away?"

"Don't worry, Isabella." Rosie told her, feeling very determined. "I'll help you make sure that doesn't happen."

Chapter Four

"That's wonderful, Rosie!" Isabella said
happily. "How can I ever thank you?
We could start by practising more often—
Sorry, am I talking too much again?"

Rosie laughed and shook her head, as she
tried to brush some more of the mud from
her clothes.

"But I'm forgetting my manners," Isabella
went on. "You must let me find you a clean
gown. Will you come back to the castle with
me?"

Rosie nodded. It would be incredibly

exciting to see Isabella's castle. "What about Cedric?" she asked.

"Oh, he's tired out after all our target practice," Isabella replied. "He'll pop back into his cave and sleep now."

Right on cue, Cedric yawned, opening his mouth wide and showing his shiny white teeth.

"I'll just tuck him up in bed," said Isabella, leading Cedric towards the cave.

Rosie followed them inside. The cave was large and warm and dry, with a huge pile of sweet-smelling hay in one corner. Rosie watched as Cedric

settled himself comfortably, then she helped
Isabella to heap the straw around him.

"There, he'll be nice and cosy now,"
Isabella declared as she dropped a kiss on
Cedric's forehead. His eyes were already
closing sleepily. "Come on, Rosie."

The two of them tiptoed out as a deep,
rumbling snore echoed around the cave.

"This way," Isabella said, leading Rosie
towards a field of golden corn, which waved
and rustled in the light breeze. "We'll go
through the village."

Rosie nodded. They threaded their way
through the cornfield and then across a green
meadow, the grass starred with buttercups
and daisies. A stream ran along the bottom
of the field, and on the other side of the
water was the village.

Rosie looked around curiously as she

crossed the narrow wooden bridge with Isabella. The village looked exactly like the pictures she had seen in storybooks. There were little cottages with thatched roofs and tiny, colourful gardens full of bright flowerbeds and neat vegetable patches. Next to the cottages were pigsties and sheep pens filled with animals. Hens scratched around in the grass, squawking and clucking, and there were plenty of people bustling about. Rosie noticed that the men wore simple shirts and breeches, while the women wore dresses with long, full skirts.

Rosie was so fascinated by the busy scene that she almost walked right into a hen which was wandering around on the grass in front of her. The hen squawked crossly and hurried off.

"Sorry!" Rosie called after it. Then she

noticed a blackened patch of grass just by
her feet. "What's this?"

Isabella blushed. "That's one of Cedric's
accidents," she explained. Then she pointed to
a tree at the side of the path. "That's
another."

Rosie glanced at the tree. The branches were black, and the leaves had been burned off.

"Oh, dear!" she said.

"And Mr Gregory's gate nearly went up in flames too," Isabella continued, pointing at one of the cottages. Rosie looked and saw that the wooden garden gate was charred and scorched. She was beginning to understand why Isabella's father and the villagers were quite upset with Cedric.

"Look over there, Rosie," Isabella said, pausing as they reached the end of the

village street. "That's my father's castle."

Rosie caught her breath as she stared at the castle on the hill. It was built of pale pink stone and there were many towers and turrets of shining gold which dazzled and glittered in the sun. A white banner flew from the top of each golden tower and cream-coloured roses rambled over the walls. It was truly the most beautiful fairytale castle that Rosie had ever seen.

"It's wonderful!" she said admiringly, as they drew closer to the magnificent building. "You're so lucky to live here, Isabella."

But Isabella was frowning. "Oh, dear, not again!" she sighed, pointing towards the front of the castle.

Rosie looked where Isabella was pointing. People were standing in line outside the castle walls. Every single one of them was

clutching something scorched or burned.
One had a cloak, another a basket of
vegetables and a third held part of a
wooden picket fence. They all looked very
annoyed indeed.

"Come this way," Isabella whispered,
taking Rosie's hand. "I don't want
them to see us."

Rosie followed her
friend towards the castle
and then down a path
that ran alongside
the thick stone wall
surrounding the
building. Soon the girls
were completely out of
sight. Then, to Rosie's
amazement, Isabella
slipped behind a tree

which grew beside the castle wall and pressed one of the pale pink stones. As she pushed, a large rectangle of stones began to move aside, leaving a gap in the castle wall.

"A secret passage!" Rosie gasped, peering inside. She saw a long, winding corridor, lit by burning wooden torches fixed to the walls.

Isabella nodded. "Follow me," she said, and slipped inside. When they were both in the corridor, she pressed a lever, and the stones slotted silently back into place.

"Who are those people?" Rosie asked as they walked down the winding corridor. "And why were they waiting outside the castle?"

"They're from the village," Isabella replied glumly. "I think they're waiting to see my father to complain about Cedric. Did you see how angry they looked?"

"Yes, I did," Rosie admitted, with a worried frown. She could understand that the villagers were annoyed about their burnt possessions, but she hoped that if Isabella was given a little time to train Cedric all the accidents would soon stop.

They were at the end of the corridor now, facing a wooden door. Isabella took a long, thin key made of wrought iron out of her sleeve and unlocked the door. To Rosie's amazement, they emerged into a cupboard hung with silk, satin and velvet dresses in every colour of the rainbow.

"This is my wardrobe," Isabella announced. She pushed the clothes aside and opened the wardrobe doors. "And this is my bedchamber."

Rosie stepped out into the room and looked around, her eyes wide. There was a

four-poster bed, draped with curtains of pure white silk, and at the end of it stood a long, carved wooden bench piled with satin cushions. Woven rugs covered the stone floor and the walls were hung with tapestries.

Isabella ran to the enormous arched window and peered out over the balcony. "I've never seen so many villagers come to complain all at once!" she sighed. "Oh, Rosie, I'm so worried. What if they manage to convince my father that I must get rid of Cedric? This might make up his mind once and for all!"

Rosie didn't know what to say. She felt sorry for Isabella and Cedric; things were indeed looking bad for the gentle dragon.

Chapter Five

"Maybe we should go and listen to what the villagers are saying to your father," Rosie suggested. "Then we can make sure we speak up for Cedric."

Isabella nodded. "That's a good idea," she said. "But first I'll find you a clean dress." She sorted through the clothes in her wardrobe and drew out a pretty pink silk gown embroidered with silver flowers. Rosie couldn't believe how beautiful it was. She slipped out of her muddy gold dress and Isabella helped her into the clean pink one.

"Now, let's go and find out what's happening," Isabella said eagerly. "Cedric has no one to stand up for him except me."

"And me!" Rosie added firmly, and Isabella smiled gratefully at her.

The two girls hurried out of Isabella's bedchamber and down a wide, winding set of stairs. The passageways of the castle were hung with tapestries and lit with flaming torches.

"My father will be receiving the villagers in the Great Hall," Isabella panted as she led the way along yet another corridor. "If we go up to the Minstrels' Gallery, where the musicians sit and play at feasts, we'll have a really good view of what's going on."

Isabella ran up a final set of stairs and drew back a velvet curtain. Rosie looked

around curiously as she followed her
new friend onto a long wooden balcony
overlooking the Great Hall. Musical
instruments, such as lutes, pipes and flutes,
lay upon velvet cushions here and there
on the floor, along with other instruments
which Rosie didn't recognize.

Isabella put her finger to her lips and
she and Rosie tiptoed to the front of the
gallery. Rosie was careful not to trip over
any of the instruments and make a noise
which would give away their hiding-place.

They were standing above a huge hall,
hung with colourful banners stretching
from floor to ceiling. At one end was a
raised platform, upon which were two
golden thrones. Isabella's father, the king,
sat on one of them and her mother, the
queen, on the other. The king was tall and

stately with a neatly trimmed black beard, while the queen had the same fair hair and blue eyes as Isabella. In front of them, in an orderly queue, stood the villagers the girls had seen outside the castle gates and two guards in smart red and black uniforms.

"Thank you, Mrs Merriwether," the king was saying to a grumpy-looking woman in a red dress. "I have noted your complaint and I am sorry that you have had so much trouble."

Isabella turned to Rosie. "That's the woman who owns the village laundry," she whispered. "Cedric happened to pass by the wet clothes hanging on her washing line and accidentally made them just a *little* bit drier than they were supposed to be!"

Rosie giggled and bit her lip. She looked down at Mrs Merriwether, who was holding the charred remains of what looked like a shirt and a pair of trousers.

"Farmer George?" the king said, looking at the next person in line.

The farmer stepped forwards, looking very annoyed. "All the corn in my field has been cooked before I even got the chance to harvest it, Your Majesty! It was that dragon again!"

The king shook his head, now looking rather annoyed himself. "I must sort this matter out once and for all!" he sighed, his face serious. "Isabella! *Isabella!*"

"Oh, dear!" Isabella's face fell. "This looks bad, Rosie. I must go down and speak to my father right away. Do you want to wait here?"

"No, I'll come with you," Rosie said bravely. "Maybe I can help you persuade your father to give Cedric another chance."

The guards stood aside to let Isabella and Rosie pass into the Great Hall through the big wooden doors. Everyone in the hall was gossiping about Cedric's latest adventures, but they fell silent as the girls entered. Rosie felt very nervous.

"Isabella, my child, come here." The king held out his hand and his gaze fell on Rosie. "Who is this?"

"My friend, Lady Rosalind, Father," Isabella replied.

Rosie tried not to laugh. She'd never been called a lady before!

"You are very welcome here, Lady Rosalind," said the king politely. Rosie curtseyed low, sneaking a look at Isabella's father as she did so. He had a kind face and a pleasant smile, but he did look rather annoyed. The queen was frowning, too.

"Father, please let me say sorry to the villagers for the damage that Cedric has caused," Isabella began anxiously. "I know his fire-breathing still isn't quite under control. But he's practising hard and he *is* getting better."

"I'm sorry, my dear." The king shook his head. "But I simply cannot allow this to continue any longer."

Isabella's eyes filled with tears and she turned to her mother.

"Your father's right, dear," the queen said gently.

"That dragon is nothing but trouble," the king announced. "And I am tired of listening to complaints about him every day." He frowned, stroking his beard. "My dear, I really think it's time—"

Rosie had been racking her brains, trying

to think of something she could say to help Cedric. But suddenly her thoughts and the king's words were both interrupted by the sound of someone running towards the Great Hall. And then everyone heard a man's voice in the corridor outside, shouting, "Fire! The village bakery's on fire!"

Chapter Six

Everyone in the Great Hall gasped with horror. Rosie glanced at Isabella and knew she was thinking the same thing. Had Cedric woken up, wandered down to the village and accidentally set fire to the bakery?

The guards opened the doors of the Great Hall and a man rushed in. He was red in the face and panting. "Fire, Your Majesty!" he yelled. "The whole bakery's going up in flames!"

Everyone, courtiers and villagers alike, poured out of the castle and headed for the village. Rosie followed them with Isabella and the king and queen. As they hurried out of the castle, they could see plumes of grey smoke billowing up into the blue sky.

"Oh, Rosie, I'm scared," Isabella whispered as they rushed down the path to the village. "What if this is Cedric's fault?"

"Maybe it isn't," Rosie said, trying to cheer Isabella up. "Something else could have started the fire."

Isabella nodded but she didn't look much happier. As they crowded into the main square, Rosie could see great clouds of smoke and feel the burning heat of the fire. The bakery, a low wooden building, stood on one side of the square. Flames were leaping out of the windows, burning higher and higher as the fire took hold. There was a choking smell of burning bread in the air, and people began to cough.

Suddenly a gust of wind blew up and swirled around the square. It fanned the flames, sending them shooting across the bakery roof, dangerously close to the cottage next door.

"We must put this out before it spreads!" the king shouted, taking charge of the situation. "Everyone go and fetch as many buckets as you can find. We'll make a chain to the stream, and bring water that way."

The crowd broke up as people fled in all directions to do the king's bidding. When a pile of buckets had been collected, Isabella and Rosie joined the chain of people

between the stream and the bakery and began passing buckets back and forth. It was hard work. Rosie's back ached and soon her clothes were wet. But everyone kept going until, at long last, the flames had been put out.

"The bakery's ruined," Isabella whispered to Rosie, staring at the charred remains of the wooden building. "It will have to be rebuilt."

"Well done, everyone!" the king declared gratefully. "Your bravery and hard work have stopped the fire from spreading."

"Your Majesty!" A short, round woman wearing a white apron, now black with soot, hurried forwards. "Your Majesty, what about my bakery?"

"Ah, Mrs Bunn, I'm very sorry this has happened," the king said sadly. "But please do not worry yourself. We will help you to build a new bakery with a better oven."

"There was nothing wrong with my *old* oven, Your Majesty," Mrs Bunn said firmly, folding her arms. "It was that dragon. He set my bakery on fire!"

"Oh, no!" Isabella whispered, clutching Rosie's hand.

"That dragon's a pest," Mrs Bunn went on, wiping her sooty hands on her apron. "And it's time something was done about him, Your Majesty."

There was a murmur of agreement from the crowd. Rosie and Isabella turned to the king, their faces anxious.

"You're right, Mrs Bunn," the king sighed.

"I must do something I should have done a long time ago."

"Father!" Isabella stepped forward and touched his arm. "Father, please!"

The king looked down at her and shook his head.

Then the queen took Isabella's hand and pulled her away gently. "It's for the best, dear," she murmured.

Rosie watched unhappily as Isabella's eyes filled with tears. Was there nothing they could do? "Isabella, don't cry," she whispered. "If we put our heads together, maybe we can come up with a plan."

The king raised his hand. "Send for the knight!" he proclaimed.

The villagers immediately took up the cry. "Send for the knight! Send for the knight!"

"Who's the knight?" Rosie asked Isabella.

"And what is he going to do?"

"He lives here in the village," Isabella said sadly. "He'll drive Cedric far away from the kingdom, where he can do no more harm." Her voice wobbled. "And I'll never see him again!"

"My dear, please don't be sad," the king said to Isabella, looking very upset himself. "Cedric is dangerous, and I have to protect the kingdom. There is nothing else I can do."

There was a loud fanfare of trumpets and the villagers turned their heads as the sound of hoof beats echoed around the town square. The next moment, a beautiful white horse cantered into view, tossing its long white mane.

On the horse's back sat a tall knight in shining silver armour. He looked very noble but Rosie saw that in one hand he

carried a fearsome, pointed lance, and
she wondered how she and Isabella could
possibly save Cedric.

Chapter Seven

"Hurrah!" the villagers shouted joyfully. They took off their hats and waved them in the air and the children jumped up and down, clapping their hands with glee. Rosie could see that everyone looked very relieved and pleased to see the knight, except for herself and Isabella, of course.

"Do you know how many dragons he's banished?" a man whispered to the woman standing next to him.

Rosie leaned a little closer so that she could hear.

"Twelve!" the man continued. "And one was twice as big as Cedric."

"Isn't he handsome?" the woman sighed, as the knight raised the visor on his helmet and waved at the crowd.

Rosie couldn't help thinking that the knight did seem rather impressive as he slid out of the saddle and leaped to the ground.

"Your Majesty!" he announced in ringing tones. "Have no fear; I am here!" He swept off his helmet and bowed before the king and queen.

Then he turned to Isabella. "Ah, the beautiful Princess Isabella!" he said. "May I?" He tried to take Isabella's hand.

Rosie couldn't help smiling when she saw the look on Isabella's face and the way she tried to hide her hands behind her back. The knight managed to get hold of one of them and kissed it loudly. Isabella pulled a face at Rosie and wiped her hand on her dress.

"I have fought with many dragons," the knight proclaimed proudly. "Time and again I have used my skill, cunning and bravery to defeat them, banish them and stop them causing trouble for honest townsfolk."

The villagers cheered loudly at this.

"Prepare a great feast for me!" the knight continued, raising his lance high in the air. "For tomorrow I shall face the dragon and drive it from the land!"

There were more cheers.

"I shall order my servants to prepare a magnificent feast right away," the king agreed. "It will be held tonight, in the castle gardens, and everyone is invited."

"But no strawberries at the feast, please," the knight said to the king in a low voice. "Strawberries bring me out in a rash."

"Sir Knight!" Mrs Bunn stepped forwards, beaming at him. "My husband and son are at sea with the other fishermen and they will bring back the freshest of fish, just for you."

"Urgh! No fish!" The knight pulled a face. "Fish give me a tummy-ache." He stared at his reflection in the shiny surface of his helmet, tilting his head this way and that. "And I'll need a barber to give my beard a trim. I must look my best."

Rosie tried not to laugh. The knight might *look* impressive but she'd never met anyone so pompous and ridiculous!

"Rosie," Isabella whispered, as the knight rode off towards the castle, followed by the crowd of cheering villagers. "What are we going to do?"

Rosie thought fast. "We must warn Cedric," she whispered. "He'll have to find somewhere to hide, so that the knight can't drive him away."

"Good idea," Isabella whispered back. "Let's go."

The girls hung back as the crowd of people hurried after the knight. They were about to sneak off in the opposite direction to go and find Cedric, when someone called their names.

"Isabella! Lady Rosalind!"

Isabella's mother was standing on the edge of the crowd, frowning at them. "Where are you going?" she asked. "Isabella, I need you and your friend to be good hostesses and entertain the knight. Now, come along."

Rosie and Isabella glanced at each other in dismay, but they had no choice but to follow everyone else back to the castle.

"We need to slip away and warn Cedric!" Isabella muttered anxiously.

"Let's wait until the feast starts," suggested Rosie. "Then there'll be so much happening, nobody will notice we're gone."

"I hope you're right," Isabella said, looking worried.

The castle was a hive of activity. The cooks were baking, roasting, grilling and frying in the enormous kitchens. The maids were laying tables in the gardens. The musicians were tuning their instruments, and other servants were carrying chairs outside, decorating the trees with banners and lighting candles.

"Girls!" the queen called, seeing them outside the Great Hall. "Go inside and entertain our guest, the knight."

Isabella pulled a face at Rosie but they did as the queen had asked. The knight was stretched out in front of the blazing fire, toasting his toes. He looked very pleased to see them.

"Sit down, Your Highness and the Lady Rosalind!" he said. "Let me amaze and enthral you with tales of all the dragons I have defeated!"

Rosie and Isabella sat down and listened politely as the knight launched into a long and very dull story.

"And then I charged up to him on my horse and said, 'Dragon, you must leave this kingdom forthwith!'" the knight told Rosie and Isabella pompously. "And do you know what he did? He breathed fire at me, and singed the white feather on top of my helmet! Now that made me *really* cross!"

Rosie felt a huge yawn coming and put her hand over her mouth to hide it. She glanced at Isabella, who looked just as bored. The knight never seemed to stop boasting. Did he *ever* shut up?

"Hey, you!" The knight summoned a servant who was rushing towards the gardens carrying a large silver dish. "Take my armour away and give it a good clean. I want to be able to see my face in it."

"Yes, sire," the servant gasped, with a bow.

The knight began to take off his armour and Rosie turned to Isabella.

"Does he ever stop talking?" she whispered.

"I don't think so," Isabella replied quietly. "I expect he just bores the dragons until they can't wait to get away!"

"Now, where was I?" the knight said as the servant staggered away with his armour. "Ah, yes, I was telling you about the dragon which—"

"I'm sorry, but we must go and get ready for the feast," Isabella said quickly. "Please excuse us."

"Of course." The knight bowed. "I'll finish the story later. I've got lots more to tell you."

"That's what we're afraid of!" Rosie groaned as the two girls left the hall.

Isabella laughed as they hurried upstairs to her bedchamber. They quickly changed their dresses and brushed their hair. As they were getting ready, they heard the sound of music down in the castle gardens.

"It's getting dark and the villagers are arriving," Isabella said, looking out of the window. "It's time for the feast to start."

"Good!" Rosie said firmly. "That means we'll soon be able to get away."

"Yes," Isabella agreed. "We'll stay for a while and look like we're enjoying the feast, then slip away when nobody's looking."

By the time the two girls ran downstairs, the feast was in full swing. The musicians were playing a merry tune and people were dancing across the grass in the candlelight. The knight sat next to the king and queen, holding a silver goblet in his hand and wearing his newly polished armour.

"Tomorrow all your troubles will be over!" he declared. "The dragon will be banished, and you will see that I am the best, the bravest and

the handsomest knight in all of Tannelaun!"

"The most conceited, too!" Rosie murmured to Isabella.

The girls giggled and hurried away so the knight wouldn't notice. They mingled with the villagers who were feasting and dancing. The food looked delicious but Rosie was too worried about Cedric to eat anything. She was just wondering if she and Isabella would ever get the chance to slip away and see the dragon, when the king rose to his feet.

"Please gather round," he called. "The court jesters and tumblers will now entertain you."

"Perfect!" Rosie whispered to Isabella as men in brightly coloured, diamond-patterned costumes ran out onto the grass and began to juggle and tumble. "Let's go."

"Wait!" Isabella said. "Can you hear something?"

Rosie listened hard. Over the sound of the music she could just make out a low grumble of thunder. She glanced up. The sky had turned a deep, threatening purple and the moon was completely blotted out by clouds. The torches lighting the feast started to flicker and go out and, as Rosie stared upwards, she felt a drop of rain splash on her face.

"There's going to be a storm!" she gasped.

Other people were staring up at the sky now. Suddenly a jagged flash of silver lightning seared the clouds and the rain began to fall faster and faster.

"Quickly!" the king shouted. "Everyone take cover in the castle."

"This rain is going to dull the shine on my armour!" the knight moaned, pushing people aside in his hurry to get out of the downpour.

"Girls!" the queen called, seeing Rosie and Isabella hesitating as everyone else rushed inside. "What are you doing? You're getting soaked! Come in right away!"

Reluctantly, Rosie and Isabella did as they were told.

"What a shame," sighed the queen as everyone gathered in the Great Hall. "We were having such a lovely feast."

"Someone bring a cloth," the knight called in panic, "and polish the raindrops off my armour!"

Just then, a blinding flash of lightning lit up the hall. It was closely followed by a deafening thunderclap that made everyone gasp.

"What about the fishermen?" Mrs Bunn said suddenly. "They're still out in their boats."

"This is not a night to be at sea," the king agreed, looking grave. "Let us hope they are on their way back into the harbour."

"Well, I must go and see if my husband and my son are safe!" Mrs Bunn said anxiously.

There were murmurs of agreement from the other villagers and soon everyone was pulling on their jackets and hats and rushing out into the driving rain, heading for the harbour. The king and queen wrapped themselves in hooded cloaks and followed. Rosie and Isabella did the same.

"I hope all the fishermen have made it home safely," Isabella said as they hurried along. Rosie could hardly hear what she was saying, though, as another great roar of thunder sounded overhead and the wind howled around them.

Down on the beach, the wind was even

stronger. Rosie huddled deeper into her
warm woollen cloak as she and Isabella
followed the crowd across the wet sand.

"The boats aren't back!" Mrs Bunn
shouted, staring around the harbour. She
scanned the raging sea anxiously. "They
must still be out there!"

Rosie peered through the wind and the
rain. The moon was still hidden behind the
clouds, making the darkness pitch-black.
The only things Rosie could make out were
the white horses on the crests of the huge
waves that thundered towards the beach.

But then, all of a sudden, Rosie thought

she glimpsed a light out on the sea. "Look!" she called. "There's a light out there!"

"It's one of the boats' lanterns!" Isabella cried. "See, there are four of them!"

Rosie stared hard at the pinpricks of light as they were tossed this way and that. Gradually she made out the shapes of four fishing boats. She could also see that the safe waters of the harbour were surrounded by tall, jagged black rocks and the boats were being hurled closer and closer towards them.

"We must do something!" Mrs Bunn cried, clasping her hands in despair. "Otherwise the boats will be wrecked on the rocks, and the men will drown!"

Chapter Eight

"How fortunate that we have the knight to help us!" declared the king, turning to the knight, who had just ridden up on his white horse. "Sir Knight, what would you suggest? What can you do to save our fishermen?"

"Me?" The knight looked extremely shocked and he dismounted hurriedly. "Your Majesty, give me a dragon and I'm your man. But I can't swim or sail a boat!"

The king and queen stared at him in horror, while the villagers looked very disappointed and began muttering to each other. Rosie raised her eyebrows at Isabella and shook her head. The knight wasn't turning out to be much help.

"We must find a way to guide the boats safely between the rocks at the mouth of the harbour," one of the village men shouted.

"Yes, we need some light," the king agreed.

"But, Your Majesty, it is too wet to make a spark," declared a servant.

"Not necessarily," Rosie murmured thoughtfully. "Isabella, is there a way we can use Cedric's fiery breath to light some sort of beacon to guide the boats?"

"That's a great idea, Rosie!" Isabella declared. She thought for a moment and then clapped her hands. "Look, up there on the cliff!"

Rosie glanced up. On the edge of the towering cliff she saw a dead tree, its leafless branches outlined starkly against the night sky. All they needed to do was get Cedric to set light to it.

"Quickly, Rosie!" Isabella urged, grabbing her hand and leading her off across the beach. "We must get Cedric right away!"

Luckily, Rosie realized, everyone else was too busy staring at the boats to notice them leaving. "But have we got time to get to Cedric's cave before the boats hit the rocks?" she panted, as she followed Isabella across the wet sand.

"We have if we go on horseback!" Isabella replied. She rushed over to the knight's charger and lightly swung herself up into the saddle. Then she leaned down and helped pull Rosie up behind her. "Let's go, boy," she whispered in the horse's ear. "Hang on, Rosie!"

The horse galloped swiftly off across the beach, with Isabella holding the reins and

Rosie clutching tightly to Isabella.

"Hey, that's my horse!" the knight shouted
indignantly behind them. "Stop, thieves!"

But Isabella simply urged the horse to go
faster. They flew through the village, across
the fields and up to the entrance of Cedric's
cave. The dragon was peering out through
the rain and his soft brown eyes lit up when
he saw Isabella and Rosie.

"Cedric, we need your help!" Isabella
called, slipping off the horse's back and
beckoning to Cedric.

Immediately the dragon padded out of the cave and stared eagerly at Isabella. Rosie could see that he understood what her friend was saying.

Isabella carefully tethered the horse inside the dragon's cave and then leaped onto Cedric's back just as easily as she had mounted the knight's horse. "Climb aboard, Rosie!" she cried.

Rosie followed a little more cautiously. She reached out and pulled herself up onto Cedric, settling herself down on the smooth golden scales between his wings.

"Cedric, take us to the harbour," Isabella said.

"And please go as fast as you can!" Rosie added, then caught her breath as Cedric unfolded his enormous golden wings.

With a couple of powerful wing beats, the dragon rose into the air and set off towards the village.

"Hurry, Cedric!" Isabella called.

The dragon soared through the dark, rainy skies towards the harbour, as Rosie and Isabella clung to his neck. Rosie could hardly believe that she was actually riding on a dragon's back!

They were flying at quite a speed, and Rosie could feel her hair streaming out behind her. She crouched down lower, wiping the rain from her face. But despite the wind that whistled past Rosie's ears, Cedric felt as steady as a rock.

"Cedric's much quicker than the horse," Rosie called to Isabella, as they reached the harbour only a few minutes later.

Rosie could see that the fishing boats were still in trouble out on the stormy sea. She looked down at the beach. Some of the villagers had brought candles and lanterns but they were having trouble lighting them in the heavy wind and rain. Isabella urged Cedric on until they reached the cliff top and Rosie saw the dead tree that Isabella had pointed out to her.

"Do you think Cedric will be able to set

fire to the tree?" she asked her friend hopefully.

"I'm sure he will!" Isabella replied. She leaned forwards and spoke into the dragon's ear. "Now, Cedric, you see that old tree? I need you to breathe fire at it."

Rosie clung on, watching anxiously as Cedric circled the tree, his big brown eyes fixed on his target. He didn't seem too nervous. Rosie thought that perhaps he hadn't noticed the villagers down on the beach because of the storm and the rain. As Cedric opened his mouth, Rosie took a deep breath. This *had* to work!

Then she heard a distant cry.

"Look!" One of the villagers on the beach had glanced up and spotted Cedric circling overhead. "It's the dragon! What's he doing?"

For an awful moment, Rosie thought that

the villager's cry might distract
Cedric. But the dragon had
already breathed out
a stream of fire.
The flames
whooshed
through the
wind and the
rain, straight
towards the
brittle branches
of the tree.
They hit it
right in the centre and
immediately it began to blaze.

"Well done, Cedric!" Rosie
gasped. "You did it!"

"I knew he could!" said Isabella proudly,
patting Cedric's neck.

Cedric raised his head and stared wide-eyed at the burning tree. He looked very pleased with himself.

There were cheers from the villagers on the beach below. As Cedric hovered high above the burning tree, keeping his distance from the flames, Rosie and Isabella stared out to sea. They could see that the fishermen were now trying to guide their boats through the gap in the rocks, towards the flaming beacon and the safety of the harbour.

It was a struggle but one of the boats eventually managed to make its way in towards the shore, followed by two of the others.

"Three of the boats are coming safely into the harbour!" the king cried in relief, and the wind carried his words to the girls on the cliff.

"But look!" Mrs Bunn wailed, her eyes fixed on the fourth boat. "That's my husband's, the *Mary Anne*. It's too far past the harbour mouth and it's heading for the rocks!"

Rosie watched in dismay. Mrs Bunn was right. The *Mary Anne* had become separated from the other boats and though its crew could now see the way they should go, it was too late for them to change course.

There was a loud and terrible crunch as the small wooden boat struck a jagged rock, and began to break into pieces on the stormy sea.

Chapter Nine

"Oh, no!" Mrs Bunn exclaimed. "What are we going to do?"

"Isabella, do you think Cedric could rescue the fishermen from the boat?" Rosie asked urgently.

Isabella nodded. "I think so," she replied. "Quickly, Cedric, fly down to the boat! We need to bring the crew safely ashore."

The dragon whirled round in the air and headed out across the raging sea, still carry-ing Rosie and Isabella on his back. The wind was stronger out here and Rosie could feel salty spray on her face. Cedric's wings were flapping a little harder than before, but he still felt strong and steady.

He hovered above the broken fishing boat and Rosie and Isabella looked down. They could see three men and a young boy trying to scramble out of the disintegrating boat and onto the slippery rocks.

"Mr Bunn!" Isabella shouted. "Up here! Cedric will save you!"

Mr Bunn glanced upwards and his eyes nearly popped out of his head when he saw the golden dragon above him.

"Take my son first!" he cried, lifting the boy up.

"Cedric, be very careful," breathed Rosie anxiously as the dragon flew downwards.

Cedric stopped a little way above the young boy. Then he opened his mouth, and

gently took the collar
of the boy's jacket
in his teeth. He
lifted him off the
wrecked boat,
and flew
quickly back
to the shore.

"Edward!" wept
Mrs Bunn, as Cedric
placed her son carefully on the sand and
soared up into the air again. "You're safe!"

"Now for the others, Cedric," said Isabella.
The dragon flew back to the boat. The
other men, including Mr Bunn, were heavier
than Edward and Cedric had to use his
teeth and his claws to pick them up. But he
managed it very carefully, taking each man
to the safety of the beach and then flying

back for the next. Soon Cedric was heading back to shore, carrying Mr Bunn, the last man from the boat. The dragon landed on the beach and dropped Mr Bunn gently onto the sand.

"Well done, Cedric!" said the king, as Mrs Bunn hugged her husband. All the villagers cheered and Isabella and Rosie beamed at each other.

"Now, everyone back to the castle where we can all get warm and dry!" directed the queen.

"Wasn't Cedric great?" said Rosie happily. "He was a real hero. And he didn't have one fiery hiccup!"

"I think it was because he didn't have time to be scared," replied Isabella. "Maybe he's cured! I hope so. Then my father might let me keep him."

Cedric beamed at the two girls and yawned sleepily.

"Come back to the castle with us, Cedric," said Isabella, patting his head. "I'll find you a nice, warm place to sleep."

The girls followed everyone else back to the castle. With the help of one of the stable-hands, they settled Cedric on a cosy bed of straw in a loosebox, while one of the grooms rushed off to fetch the knight's charger from Cedric's cave.

Rosie and Isabella were just drying off in front of the fire in Isabella's bedchamber, when a servant came to the door.

"Please, Your Highness," she said, "the king wants to see you straight away."

Isabella gave Rosie an anxious look. "Oh, dear," she sighed. "That doesn't sound good."

Rosie felt nervous too as she and Isabella

hurried to the Great Hall. The king and queen were seated on their thrones and the hall was packed with villagers and courtiers. Rosie was dismayed to see that the king looked rather stern.

"Well," said the king, staring at them, "what have you two got to say for yourselves? Putting your lives in danger; flying around on a dragon!"

Rosie glanced at Isabella and then stared at her feet, feeling very embarrassed.

"And after I told you that the dragon was dangerous and must be kept away from the village!" the king went on. "You disobeyed my orders! But I must say . . ." he added, breaking into a smile, "you were both very brave!"

Rosie and Isabella looked at each other in relief.

"Thank you, girls," he said. "If it wasn't for you, our hard-working fishermen would have drowned." Everyone in the Great Hall cheered and clapped loudly. "Lady Rosalind," the king said, turning to Rosie, "you will always be an honoured guest in our kingdom."

There was more applause and Rosie blushed.

"And Cedric the dragon is a hero too," the king added. "But we still have to remember that he has caused a great deal of damage in the village . . ."

Isabella's face fell at her father's words.

"If it was just small accidents, we could learn to live with them," the king said, putting his hand on his daughter's shoulder. "But burning down the bakery is a very serious matter. I'm afraid there is no way we can allow Cedric to remain in Tannelaun."

"I should think so too!" said the knight loudly. "As soon as I've checked my armour thoroughly for rust, I shall drive him from the kingdom!"

"No!" Isabella burst out.

"Cedric saved the fishermen!" Rosie
protested.

The king shook his head, still looking
very grave.

"Wait!" Mrs Bunn suddenly cried,
hurrying into the Great Hall. She looked
rather sheepish as she
curtseyed before the
king. "Your Majesty,
I have to tell
you . . ."

"Tell me what?"
the king asked.

Mrs Bunn
curtseyed again
and Rosie was
surprised to see that
she looked very
embarrassed indeed.

"Well . . . I forgot that I left a loaf of bread in the oven, Your Majesty," Mrs Bunn mumbled.

The king raised his eyebrows. "What are you trying to tell us, Mrs Bunn?"

"The loaf of bread must have burned to a crisp," Mrs Bunn went on, "and that's what started the fire."

"Then it wasn't Cedric's fault at all!" Isabella gasped.

Rosie turned to the king, her eyes shining. "Your Majesty, does this mean Isabella can keep Cedric after all?"

Chapter Ten

Rosie held her breath as she and Isabella stared at the king.

"Where is the dragon now?" he asked.

"In the stables, Father," Isabella replied.

The king turned to one of his servants. "Send for the dragon!" he ordered.

"Send for the dragon!" the servant shouted, running for the doors.

"Send for the dragon!" echoed the cry around the castle and everyone waited in silence until the servant returned with Cedric padding along behind him.

The dragon blinked sleepily as he stared around at all the people in the Great Hall but he didn't seem nervous.

The king turned to his daughter. "Isabella, your brave pet is welcome to stay in Tannelaun," he declared. "But you must continue his training. In fact, I appoint you Royal Dragon Trainer from this day forwards."

"Oh, Father, thank you!" Isabella cried. She flung her arms around the king and gave him a hug.

Cheers echoed around the Great Hall and everyone surged forward to pat and cuddle Cedric. But the dragon didn't look at all worried. Instead he beamed round at the villagers and rumbled with contentment.

"And Cedric will also have a special job in Tannelaun," announced the king, "for he shall light a warning beacon on stormy nights when the fishermen are out at sea."

At this, the queen stepped forward, smiling, and slipped a red silk sash over Cedric's head. On it, in gold letters, were the words OFFICIAL BEACON-LIGHTER OF TANNELAUN.

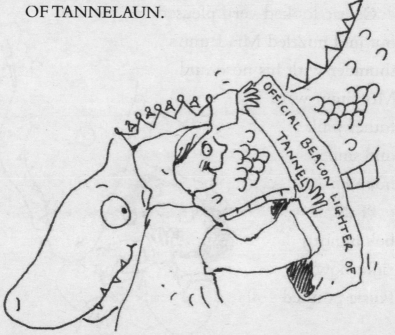

"Sir Dragon . . ." Mrs Bunn murmured nervously, stepping forward and bobbing a curtsey. "Please forgive me for blaming you for the fire. I'd like to bake your favourite cake every week to say thank you for saving my husband and son."

"Cedric loves chocolate cake," Isabella laughed.

Cedric looked very pleased. He reached out and nuzzled Mrs Bunn's shoulder with his nose and Mrs Bunn went rather pink and smiled happily.

"I think he's hungry right now," Rosie pointed

out, as Cedric licked his lips.

"Bring fruit for the noble dragon!" the king ordered his servants.

"Apples, pears and plums are his favourites," Isabella called, as the servants hurried off to the kitchen.

"And Cedric will stay here in the castle with us tonight," the king went on. "He can sleep here in the Great Hall, which is the only room big enough for him." He clapped his hands as Cedric began to yawn. "Let us all go to bed now so that the dragon can rest."

"Well, I never!" the knight said crossly, pushing his way through the crowd. "Favourite cakes! Official jobs! Sleeping in the castle! This is no way to treat a dragon. Dragons don't belong in respectable kingdoms."

"Actually, it's *you* who doesn't belong,"
said Isabella coldly.

"Well, I hardly
think . . ." blustered
the knight.

"*Goodbye*, Sir
Knight," the king
broke in with a
regal nod of his
head. "We will not
be requiring your services any longer."

The knight stalked out of the Great Hall,
looking very put out, and the villagers
headed home, chatting about the day's events
and Cedric's bravery.

As the hall emptied, Rosie and Isabella
curled up in front of the fire with Cedric and
fed him a feast of fruit. When the dragon
was full, he settled down to sleep, while the

girls rested their heads on his golden back.

"Rosie, how can I ever thank you?"
Isabella said with a yawn. "You helped me
save Cedric from that awful knight!"

"I'm so glad," replied Rosie. "And now
Cedric's getting used to the villagers, I
don't think he'll have so many accidents
from now on."

Isabella nodded sleepily. "Goodnight,
Rosie," she murmured.

Rosie smiled to herself as she stared into the orange flames. Thank goodness everything had turned out happily . . . "Goodnight, Isabella," she replied.

Suddenly, everything seemed to blur in front of Rosie's eyes and she felt herself caught up in a spinning whirlwind which whisked her through the air at top speed.

She felt herself land softly and then the winds dropped as quickly as they had sprung up. She opened her eyes. She was still in front of a fire, but it was the fire in the hall of her great-aunt's castle. And the old wooden clock on the mantelpiece had moved on just five minutes since she first started counting for hide-and-seek.

Rosie glanced up at the tapestry over the fireplace. The pompous knight had vanished, and now the little princess and the dragon

were both smiling. She felt a warm glow
and grinned to herself; what an adventure
meeting Isabella had turned out to be!

"Rosie!"

Rosie heard Luke yelling her name and

spun round to see him standing in the doorway.

"What are you doing?" he demanded.

"Aren't you supposed to be hiding?" she replied with a grin.

"Well, I found a really good hiding-place, but you didn't come!" Luke complained. "It's been *ages*. So I thought I'd come and find *you*. And you're still in here, counting!"

Rosie laughed. "OK, let's play chase instead!" she said. And with that, she dashed at Luke, who yelped in surprise and raced off down the corridor with Rosie in hot pursuit.

THE END

Did you enjoy reading about Rosie's
adventure with the Fairytale Princess?
If you did, you'll love the next
Little Princesses
book!

Turn over to read the first chapter of
The Peach Blossom Princess.

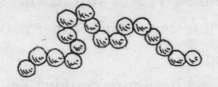

Chapter One

"Hi, Mum." Rosie said, jumping into the front seat of the car, and beaming at her mother and her younger brother. "Hi, Luke."

"You look happy," Mrs Campbell said with a smile, as she pulled away from the kerb. "So your first day at your new school went OK then?"

Rosie nodded. "It was great!" she said eagerly. "There are some nice girls in my class – I'm sitting next to one called Megan. And I really like my teacher, Miss Murray." She turned round to glance at her brother. "Did you like your teacher too, Luke?"

Luke pulled a face. "My teacher's OK," he said. "But some of the other boys said I talk funny!"

Rosie and her mum couldn't help

laughing. "That's because you don't have a Scottish accent," Mrs Campbell remarked, as she drove out of the village. "I'm sure they'll get used to you."

"Oh, I made friends with the boys who were laughing at me," Luke replied cheerfully. "We played football at lunchtime."

"Mum, Miss Murray says our class is putting on a show for the rest of the school," Rosie went on, excitedly. "It's about different countries of the world. We've each been given a country and we have to do a song, poem, dance or reading from that country."

Luke leaned forwards, looking interested. "What's your country?"

"Japan," Rosie replied. "And I don't know *anything* about Japan!"

"Japan," Luke repeated. "Is that near Scotland?"

"No, it's on the other side of the world!" Rosie laughed. "Miss Murray told everyone to look around at home for things that might be useful for the show. I bet Great-aunt Rosamund will have something!"

"Oh, yes, your great-aunt is bound to have visited Japan at some point," Mrs Campbell agreed, as she turned into the drive leading to the castle.

"I think Great-aunt Rosamund *has* been to Japan," Luke said, as the car drew to a halt.

"How do you know?" Rosie asked curiously.

Luke giggled. "I just do!" he replied, and he jumped out of the car and ran into the castle, through the large wooden door.

"He's up to something!" laughed Mrs Campbell.

"Yes, he's got that look on his face!" Rosie

agreed, and she chased after her brother.

Luke was in the Great Hall, a huge room which was packed with Great-aunt Rosamund's treasures. He had a painted fan open in his hand, and when Rosie came in, he began hopping about, twisting the fan around his face.

"Look at me!" he lisped in a girly voice. "I'm Rosie, dancing at the school show!"

Rosie pulled a face at him, but she had to laugh. "Where did you find that fan?" she asked. "It's lovely."

"It was on that table over there," Luke said, closing it up and handing it to Rosie. "I was helping Dad tidy in here one day, and he said it was Japanese."

"Maybe I could do a Japanese dance at the show, and use the fan," Rosie said thoughtfully. "I'm sure Great-aunt Rosamund wouldn't mind if I borrowed it."

Rosie decided to take the fan to her bedroom at the top of one of the castle towers and have a closer look at it. She hurried up the winding stairs, and into the pretty, round bedroom which had been her great-aunt's when she was a little girl. There Rosie stood in front of the mirror, and carefully opened the fan.

The side she was looking at was a pale sugar-pink, painted with exotic-looking birds and butterflies. Rosie struck a pose, holding the fan close to her face and peeping over the rim. Did it make her look at all Japanese?

Suddenly her heart began to race. She had just noticed the

reflection of the other side of the fan in the mirror. It was lilac-coloured and had a tree painted on it, its thin, willowy branches dotted with delicate pink blossoms. A girl sat underneath the tree, the flowers falling gently onto her raven-black hair.

"Oh!" Rosie was so surprised, she almost dropped the fan. With trembling fingers she turned it over. "Could this be another little princess?" she asked herself breathlessly.

Rosie stared down at the picture. The girl's head drooped and her eyes were sad, but she was very richly dressed in a pink kimono, patterned with white lotus flowers, and a wide silver sash.

"I'm sure she's a little princess," Rosie said, holding the fan out in front of her. "But there's only one way to find out!"

Her eyes fixed on the girl, Rosie sank

into a curtsey. "Hello!" she said, her
voice trembling with excitement.

Before Rosie had time to
catch her breath, she felt a
warm breeze shoot out of the
fan and wrap itself around
her. Sugar-pink blossom
petals swirled in the air,
and the bedroom was
filled with the sweet,
warm scent of ripe
peaches. Rosie closed her
eyes and let the whirlwind pick her up gently
and whisk her away. She couldn't wait to
find out where she was going!

Read the rest of
The Peach Blossom Princess
to follow Rosie's adventures!